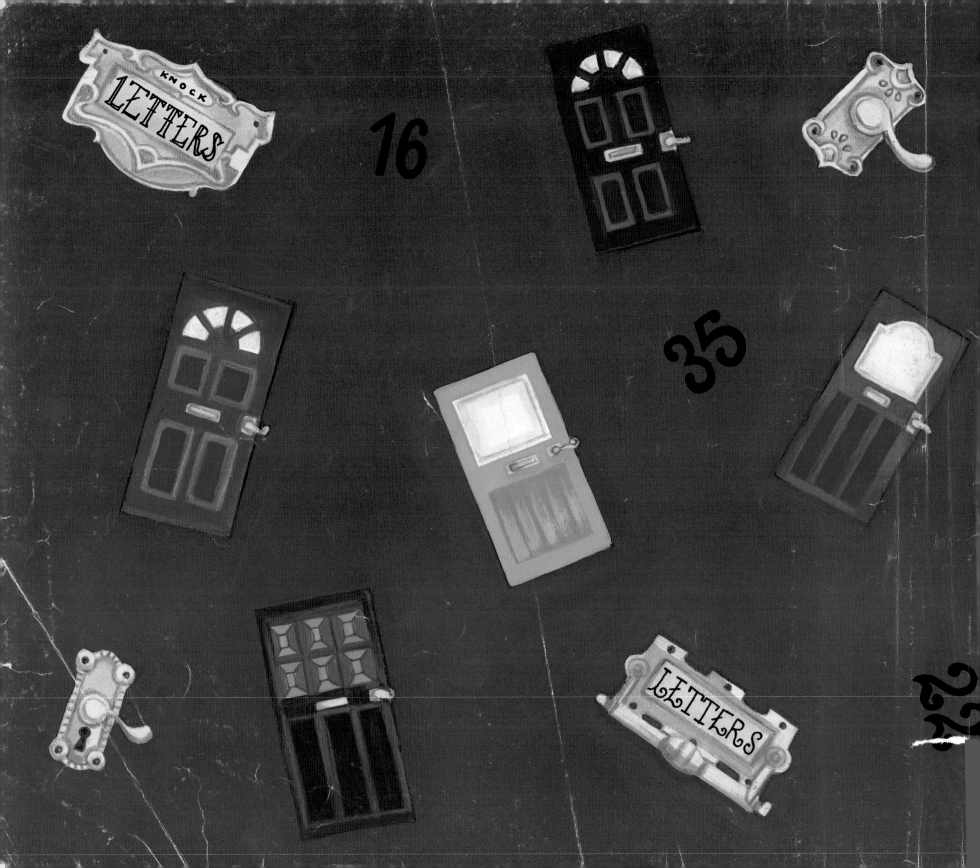

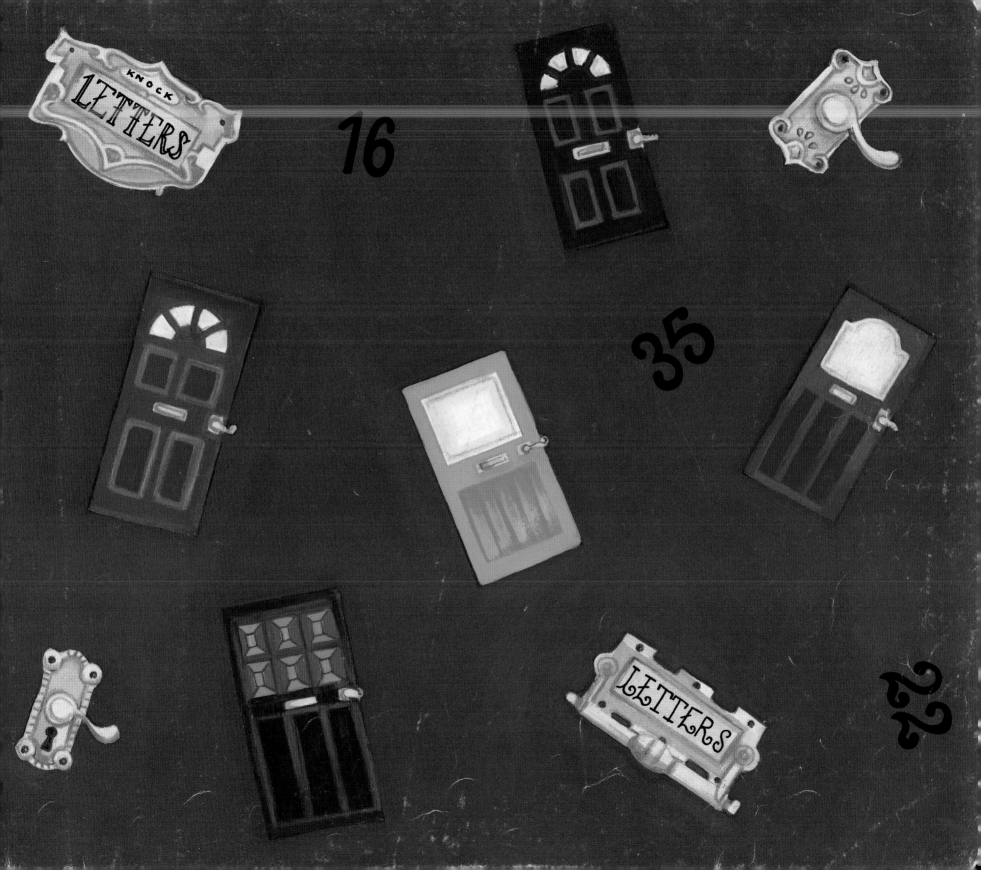

For Mum and Dad, Dave and Conrad – JH

For Mum, Gran and David (the original Davy Dark) – KW

OXFORD
UNIVERSITY PRESS

Great Clarendon Street, Oxford OX2 6DP

Oxford University Press is a department of the University of Oxford.
It furthers the University's objective of excellence in research, scholarship,
and education by publishing worldwide in

Oxford New York

Auckland Cape Town Dar es Salaam Hong Kong Karachi
Kuala Lumpur Madrid Melbourne Mexico City Nairobi
Shanghai Taipei Toronto

With offices in

Argentina Austria Brazil Chile Czech Republic France Greece
Guatemala Hungary Italy Japan Poland Portugal Singapore
South Korea Switzerland Thailand Turkey Ukraine Vietnam

Oxford is a registered trade mark of Oxford University Press in the UK and in certain other countries

British Library Cataloguing in Publication Data available

ISBN-13: 978-0-19-279201-3 (hardback)
ISBN-10: 0-19-279201-6 (hardback)
ISBN-13 978-0-19-279202-0 (paperback)
ISBN-10: 0-19-279202-4 (paperback)

10 8 6 4 2 1 3 5 7 9

Printed in China

Letterbox Lil

-a cautionary tale-

Jim Helmore & Karen Wall

OXFORD
UNIVERSITY PRESS

This is the story of
Letterbox Lil.

On the street where she lived
there is talk of her still.

By
day

or by night
from her house
she would
sneak.

And through letterboxes she'd peer and she'd peek.

If you dare to read on,

I promise to tell

of the things that Lil saw –

they may make you unwell .....

At number seven,
alert and awake,
there sits adorable
Tanya Take.

But she has
been left with
her brother's
pet snake!

Do children
taste
better

than
chocolate
cake?

Davy Dark
lives three
houses down,

in bright sunlight
he wears a frown.

By night
he's the happiest
boy in town:

with two
pointed teeth
and a
vampire's
gown!

And next door
to Davy,
Professor Biscotti

is changing
a zebra from
stripy to
spotty.

Have you ever heard anything quite so potty?

I'm sure you'll agree it's decidedly dotty!

Then Letterbox Lil
spied on
Long-Legged
Peter.

His looks
and his clothes
could not
have been neater.

But don't be misled:
he's a sly
spider-eater!

His tongue
at full

Stretch

measures
more than
a metre!

Lil wasn't put off
by the horrors she saw.
Spying was fun,
so she peeped more and more.

Dragons and witches
in books were a bore
when compared to what
lay behind any closed door!

Then one day
Lil opened
her last letterbox.

From the hairs
on her head ...

to the toes
in her socks,

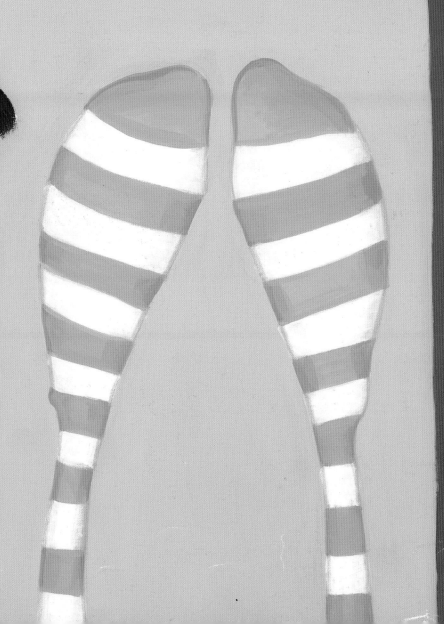

LETTERS

she was shaken
with shock,

she was frozen
with fear.

From then letterboxes
she'd never go near . . . . .

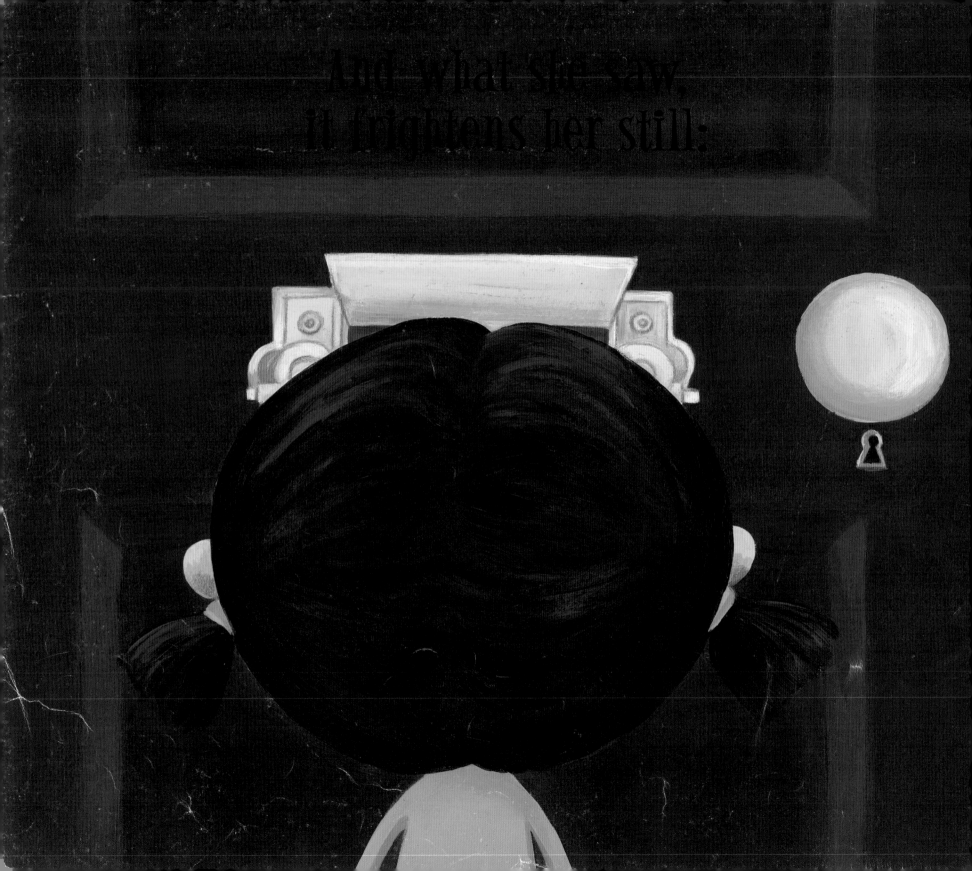

And what she saw,
it frightens her still:

So from that shocking day to this
peeping is something that Lil doesn't miss.

Spying is fun, it's undoubtedly true,
but not when the person
that's spied on
is you!

And this, my friends,
concludes the tale.
Good night,
sleep tight,
don't look so pale .....

'But don't finish there!' I hear you all shout.
'What looked back at Lil? We want to find out!'

A monster that roars
with slobbering jaws?

A beast from the deep
coiled up in a heap?

Or something that's loud and incredibly **smelly,** with ears on its chin and a nose in its belly?

Come close and I'll tell in the softest of whispers...

those bright eyes belonged
to sleek Willow Whiskers!

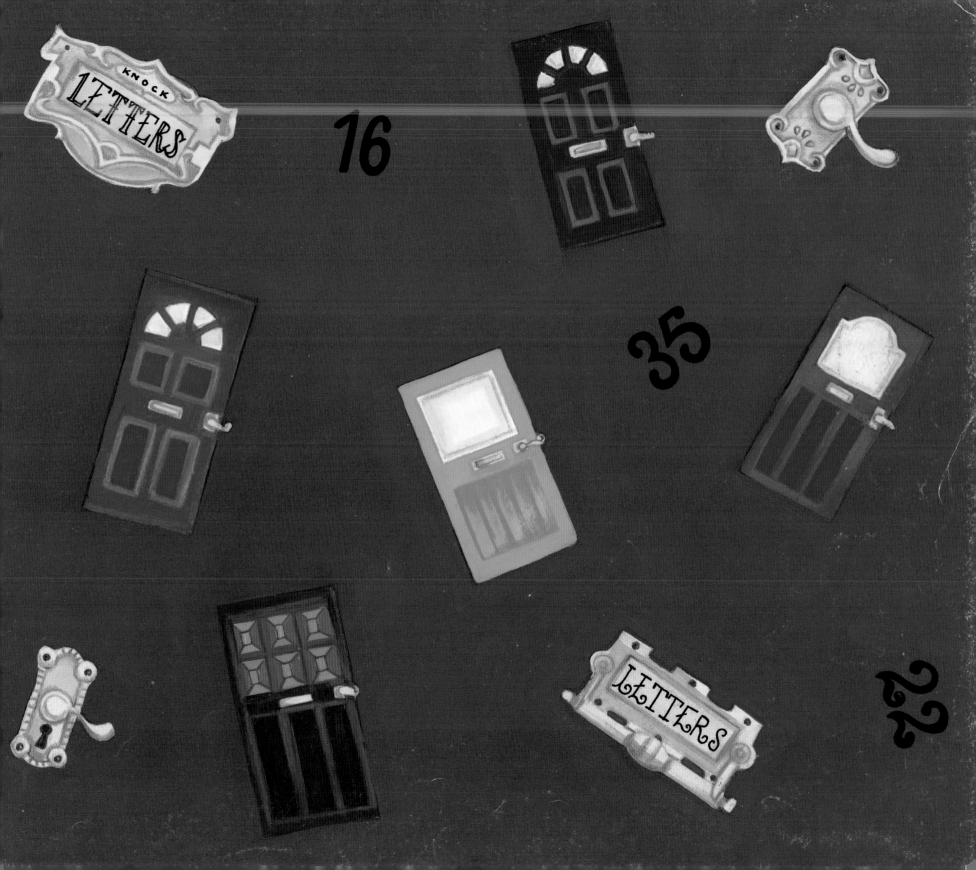